APR 16

WARRIORS

SKYCLAN & THE STRANGER

#3: AFTER THE FLOOD

WARRIORS

SKYCLAN & THE STRANGER

#3: AFTER THE FLOOD

CREATED BY
ERIN HUNTER

WRITTEN BY
DAN JOLLEY

ART BY
JAMES L. BARRY

HARPER
An Imprint of HarperCollinsPublishers

First Edition

Dear readers,

The final part of SkyClan's manga trilogy is here! When we left the gorge at the end of book two, the cats were reeling from the flood that washed away their homes. Now we see them striving to rebuild dens, restock Echosong's supply of herbs, and prove that the new SkyClan is strong enough to survive.

When I first came up with the idea of a flood in the gorge, I just wanted some kind of dramatic event around which I could build a story. But as I worked out the details, I realized that scenes like this are much too familiar in real life. All over the world, communities struggle against natural disasters, from Hurricane Katrina in the U.S. to forest fires in Australia to devastating floods in Bangladesh. This gave extra significance to what the cats in SkyClan were experiencing. Up till now, the warriors of new SkyClan have been determined to cope with every setback as if it was a chance to prove how strong they are. But the scale of this disaster is overwhelming for some of them. Remember, very few of these cats were born in a Clan. They can remember their previous lives, other ways to survive without being part of a community. Leaf-star's biggest challenge is not to rebuild the flooded dens but to make sure her Clanmates stay together.

SkyClan has to understand that the gorge is as important to their survival as the warrior code. It represents their spiritual home, the place where their ancestors walked beneath the stars. If you've read the second Warriors series, you'll recall how difficult and traumatic it was for the forest Clans to find a new home. SkyClan can't give up on the gorge without a fight!

As always, it was a delight and a privilege to be able to explore these conflicts with the help of Dan and James, the amazing talents behind the manga scripts and artwork. Thank you for reading our stories. I hope you have enjoyed them!

Best wishes always,
Erin Hunter

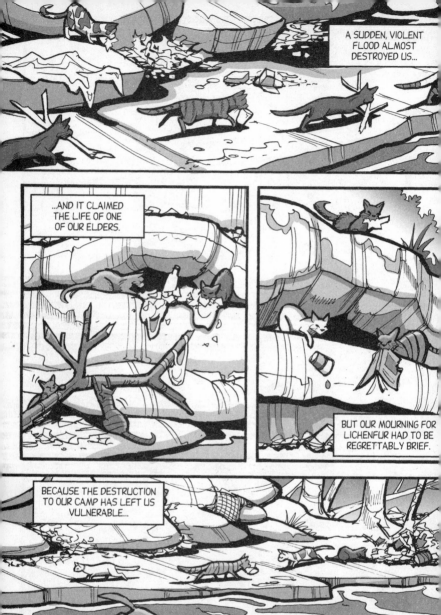

A SUDDEN, VIOLENT FLOOD ALMOST DESTROYED US...

...AND IT CLAIMED THE LIFE OF ONE OF OUR ELDERS.

BUT OUR MOURNING FOR LICHENFUR HAD TO BE REGRETTABLY BRIEF.

BECAUSE THE DESTRUCTION TO OUR CAMP HAS LEFT US VULNERABLE...

...OPEN TO ATTACKS FROM RATS...FOXES... ROGUE CATS...

...EVEN TWOLEGS.

NOT THAT OUTSIDE THREATS ARE OUR ONLY TROUBLES.

JUST AS DANGEROUS TO THE CLAN IS A LACK OF CLEAN WATER TO DRINK.

A LOT OF CARE MUST BE TAKEN AS WE REBUILD OUR CAMP.

IT REQUIRES A LOT OF THOUGHT...

...BUT EVEN MORE THAN THOUGHT RIGHT NOW, IT NEEDS A LOT OF HARD WORK AND MUSCLE.

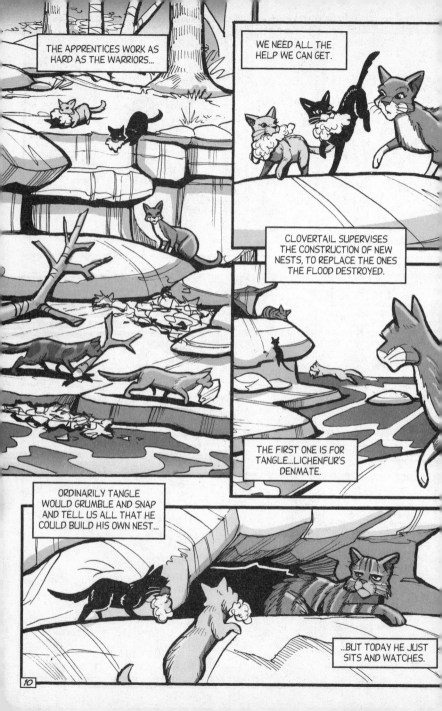

THE APPRENTICES WORK AS HARD AS THE WARRIORS...

WE NEED ALL THE HELP WE CAN GET.

CLOVERTAIL SUPERVISES THE CONSTRUCTION OF NEW NESTS, TO REPLACE THE ONES THE FLOOD DESTROYED.

THE FIRST ONE IS FOR TANGLE...LICHENFUR'S DENMATE.

ORDINARILY TANGLE WOULD GRUMBLE AND SNAP AND TELL US ALL THAT HE COULD BUILD HIS OWN NEST...

...BUT TODAY HE JUST SITS AND WATCHES.

ALMOST THERE, TANGLE! WE'LL HAVE A NEW NEST FOR YOU IN NO TIME!

I'VE GOT TO KEEP A CLOSE EYE ON HIM...

...AND TRY TO KEEP HIS GRIEF OVER LICHENFUR FROM MAKING HIM ILL.

SHARPCLAW, MY DEPUTY, HAS TAKEN CHARGE OF MOST OF THE HEAVIEST LIFTING.

I EXPECTED WASPWHISKER AND SPARROWPELT TO JOIN HIM...

...BUT HARVEYMOON TOOK ME BY SURPRISE. FOR THE LONGEST TIME I THOUGHT HE WAS THE LAZIEST CAT I HAD EVER MET.

BUT LATELY HE'S BEEN SURPRISING ME IN MORE WAYS THAN ONE.

OH-- HEY, MINTFUR...

WATCH OUT, THERE'S, UH...THERE'S THAT PUDDLE. IN FRONT OF YOU.

THANK YOU, HARVEYMOON, BUT I HAVE MADE MY WAY AROUND A PUDDLE BEFORE.

WELL, IT'S JUST--IT'S DEEPER THAN IT LOOKS. THAT'S ALL.

MY NAME IS LEAFSTAR. I AM SKYCLAN'S LEADER...

...AND EVERY CAT HERE IS MY RESPONSIBILITY.

"DON'T WORRY, LEAFSTAR," HE TELLS ME. "THE CLAN WILL REBUILD."

CAN IT REALLY BE THAT EASY?

SPLASH

I WISH TO STARCLAN I DIDN'T FEEL SO UNCERTAIN ALL THE TIME.

LEAFSTAR!

CLOVERTAIL. WHAT CAN I DO FOR YOU?

I WAS ACTUALLY WONDERING IF YOU THREE COULD HELP ME WITH A VERY IMPORTANT TASK.

OOOH! WHAT IS IT, WHAT IS IT?

WELL, WE HAVE TO CHOOSE SOME VERY NICE FEATHERS FOR TANGLE'S NEW NEST.

DO YOU THINK YOU COULD DO THAT?

I'M GREAT AT CHOOSING FEATHERS!

NUH-UH, I'M GREAT!

I'M BETTER THAN BOTH OF YOU!

I'LL PICK THE SOFTEST ONES!

15

THANK YOU.

I COULD USE A LITTLE SPACE.

OH, I KNOW WHAT KITS CAN BE LIKE.

AND I DON'T THINK TANGLE WILL MIND A FEW MORE FEATHERS IN HIS NEST.

HOW'S HE DOING?

WELL, I'M...I'M A LITTLE WORRIED.

LOSING LICHENFUR HAS HIT HIM REALLY HARD.

POP

WITH CLOVERTAIL KEEPING THE KITS OCCUPIED...

...I CAN CONCENTRATE ON PUTTING MY OWN DEN IN ORDER.

THEN FINALLY GO AND CHECK ON THE REST OF MY CLAN.

PUT YOUR BACKS INTO IT, WARRIORS!

THAT BRANCH WON'T DISLODGE ITSELF!

SHARPCLAW AND HIS MATE, CHERRYTAIL, HAVE BEEN ARGUING EVER SINCE THE FLOOD.

HE KEEPS TELLING HER SHE SHOULDN'T BE WORKING SO HARD, SINCE SHE'S EXPECTING KITS...

...AND CHERRYTAIL KEEPS TELLING HIM TO QUIT WORRYING...

...WHILE I TRY TO KEEP MYSELF FROM TEASING HIM ABOUT IT TOO MUCH.

OF COURSE, CHERRYTAIL DOES ENOUGH OF THAT FOR BOTH OF US.

WOULD YOU RELAX, SHARPCLAW?

I COULD, IF WE DIDN'T...IF YOU WEREN'T...

YOU CAN SAY IT OUT LOUD, YOU KNOW.

IT'S NOT AS IF IT'S A SECRET THAT I'M CARRYING YOUR KITS.

SHHH!

LEAFSTAR.

A MOMENT OF YOUR TIME? OR WOULD YOU RATHER TORMENT ME TOO?

OH, I'D RATHER TORMENT YOU...

...BUT I WON'T. WHAT'S ON YOUR MIND?

SO? WE DON'T EAT OUR BEDDING!

THAT'S TRUE...

...BUT JUICE FROM CRUSHED LEAVES WOULD GET IN OUR EYES.

IT WAS A GOOD IDEA, BUT I'M AFRAID IT WON'T WORK.

FINE.

YOU KNOW, I ASKED HIM TO HELP CLEAR THE STREAM, BUT HE REFUSED.

SAID HE HAD SOMETHING MORE IMPORTANT TO DO.

IF THAT WAS IT, I'M NOT IMPRESSED.

GIVE HIM A CHANCE, SHARPCLAW.

HE'S TRYING TO HELP, BUT HE HASN'T BEEN HERE LONG ENOUGH TO LEARN EVERYTHING.

HE HASN'T BEEN HERE LONG ENOUGH TO LEARN ANYTHING, BY THE LOOKS OF IT.

SOL.

WAIT A MOMENT.

UGH... THESE HERBS ARE SOGGY.

LISTEN, I WANTED TO ASK YOU... HAS STARCLAN TOLD YOU ANYTHING?

ABOUT THE FLOOD, I MEAN?

I'M AFRAID NOT. PLUS, HONESTLY, I'VE BEEN TOO BUSY TO ASK.

THE FLOOD WAS JUST ONE OF THOSE THINGS.

WHAT THINGS?

THE THINGS THAT REMIND US JUST HOW VULNERABLE WE ARE.

I DON'T SAY ANYTHING TO ECHOSONG...OR ANYONE ELSE, FOR THAT MATTER...

...BUT I FEEL A PANG OF FEAR.

WHAT IF THE SPECTER OF ANOTHER FLOOD SENDS SOME OF MY CLANMATES BACK TO THEIR OLD LIVES...

...AS LONERS OR KITTYPETS?

SPOTTEDLEAF!

I WAS BEGINNING TO WONDER IF YOU'D EVER SLEEP LONG ENOUGH TO DREAM AGAIN.

SPOTTEDLEAF-- I HAVE TO ASK YOU--

ARE WE NOT SAFE HERE ANYMORE?

DID STARCLAN SEND THE FLOOD FOR A REASON?

NO, NO, THE FLOOD WASN'T A PUNISHMENT. NOTHING LIKE THAT. BUT...

23

I GUESS THIS GOT WASHED DOWN HERE IN THE FLOOD, TOO.

I CAN'T BELIEVE WE ALL MISSED IT.

WELL, LET'S GET IT OUT OF HERE.

CAREFULLY, EVERYONE!

I CHOOSE NOT TO THINK WHAT COULD'VE HAPPENED IF THE KITS HAD DISCOVERED THIS.

MAKES ME EVEN MORE GRATEFUL FOR BILLYSTORM, AND HIS SHARP EYES.

• • •

WOW, THAT LOOKS NASTY!

IT IS.

SO STAY AWAY FROM IT, YOU THREE. I MEAN IT.

WHO KNOWS WHAT ELSE HAS BEEN WASHED DOWN?

WILL IT BE SAFE FOR OUR KITS TO PLAY IN THE GORGE?

WE CAN'T POSSIBLY CHECK EVERYWHERE!

28

THE KITS WILL BE FINE.

THEY'LL JUST HAVE TO BE CAREFUL ABOUT WHERE THEY PUT THEIR PAWS.

I TRULY BELIEVE THE KITS WILL BE FINE.

BUT TO MAKE BILLYSTORM FEEL BETTER, I LEAVE THEM WITH CLOVERTAIL FOR A BIT.

SOL, YOU MENTIONED LOOKING FOR HERBS EARLIER.

WOULD YOU LIKE ME TO SHOW YOU HOW TO FIND SOME?

THAT'D BE GREAT!

IT'S GOOD TO GET AWAY FROM THE CAMP, EVEN FOR A SHORT TIME.

AND SOL LISTENS WELL, AS I TEACH HIM SOME BASICS--HOW TO FIND MARIGOLD LEAVES, YARROW, AND COMFREY.

AND WE USE COBWEBS FOR OPEN WOUNDS.

WOW...I NEVER WOULD'VE THOUGHT OF THAT.

YOU KNOW A LOT!

WELL, LET'S SEE HOW MUCH YOU KNOW NOW.

CAN YOU FIND ME SOME YARROW ON YOUR OWN?

HERE'S SOME!

HERE'S SOME!

VERY GOOD! YOU'RE CATCHING ON QUICKLY.

SPOTTEDLEAF'S WARNING ABOUT SOL ECHOES IN MY MIND...BUT WHY?

THERE'S NOTHING SINISTER ABOUT THIS CAT.

HE'S JUST FINDING THE PATH TO BECOMING A WARRIOR A LITTLE TRICKY, THAT'S ALL.

YOU DIDN'T WARN ME ABOUT THAT, SPOTTEDLEAF!

I'M BACK.

HI, MAMA!

WHERE'S BILLYSTORM?

HE WENT ON A HUNTING PATROL!

THAT'S A NICE BIT OF MOSS.

ARE YOU STALKING IT LIKE A MOUSE?

OH, NO. IT'S OUR SPECIAL NEST!

WE'RE PRETENDING OUR HOUSEFOLK GAVE IT TO US!

YOUR... WHAT...?

BILLYSTORM SAYS WE CAN GO LIVE WITH HIM NOW! TO KEEP US SAFE IF THERE'S ANOTHER FLOOD.

YEAH! HE SAYS THE HOUSEFOLKS' DEN NEVER FLOODS!

NEVER EVER!

34

OH...HE SAID ALL THAT, DID HE?

YEAH! HE SAID IT WASN'T SAFE FOR US TO PLAY IN THE GORGE ANYMORE.

HE TOLD US ALL ABOUT THAT NASTY SILVERTHORN.

HE SAID IT WAS EVEN WORSE THAN BRAMBLES! I DON'T WANT TO HURT MY PAWS!

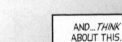

I DON'T TRUST MYSELF TO SPEAK. NOT YET.

BETTER TO WAIT.

AND... *THINK* ABOUT THIS.

UH-OH.

THUD

35

SOL! I NEED YOU TO STAY ON TASK HERE!

BUT I'VE PICKED UP A SCENT!

TURNS OUT HE'S RIGHT— I SMELL AN UNFAMILIAR CAT.

SEEMS TO HAVE WALKED ALL THE WAY ALONG OUR BORDER. MAYBE CHECKING THE MARKS?

NO ONE'S SPOTTED ANY LONERS AROUND LATELY, HAVE THEY?

I DON'T THINK SO.

HMMM. IT FADES OUT HERE.

WHAT IS THIS PLACE?

WE MAKE SURE THE BORDER MARKS ARE STRONG ALONG THE WAY...AND THAT THERE ARE NO OTHER SCENTS OF INTRUDERS.

THAT MUST HAVE BEEN A PASSING LONER WE SCENTED...

BUT STILL, KEEP ALERT WHILE YOU'RE ON PATROL.

WILL DO.

BILLYSTORM DOESN'T COME TO THE CAMP THE NEXT DAY, EITHER.

BUT I CAN'T FALTER. I CAN'T RELENT.

THE CLAN NEEDS ME TO BE STRONG NOW, MORE THAN EVER.

WHY ISN'T BILLYSTORM HERE, MAMA?

IS HE MAD AT US?

DID WE DO SOMETHING WRONG?

HE DIDN'T STOP LOVING US, DID HE?

46

LEAFSTAR-- ARE YOU BUSY RIGHT NOW?

NOT REALLY. WHY?

NO, OF COURSE NOT!

HE ISN'T ANGRY WITH YOU, AND HE WILL COME SEE YOU AGAIN. AND HE LOVES YOU ALL. VERY MUCH.

I THOUGHT YOU MIGHT LIKE TO TAKE A STROLL THROUGH THE WOODS. MAYBE CATCH A SPARROW OR TWO.

AND TALK.

IF YOU WANT TO.

I SUPPOSE THE KITS CAN'T GET INTO TOO MUCH MISCHIEF...

AND A WALK WOULD BE NICE.

DON'T GO WANDERING OFF BY YOURSELVES, YOU HEAR ME?

OKAY, MAMA!

WE WON'T!

I'M A FLOOD! YOU BETTER GET OUT OF MY WAY!

OH NO!

RUN!

47

I'M LOST IN A FOG OF MIND-NUMBING TERROR.

NO, I HAVEN'T SEEN THEM.

EVERY CAT IN THE CAMP REMEMBERS SEEING THEM...BUT NO ONE KNOWS WHERE THEY ARE.

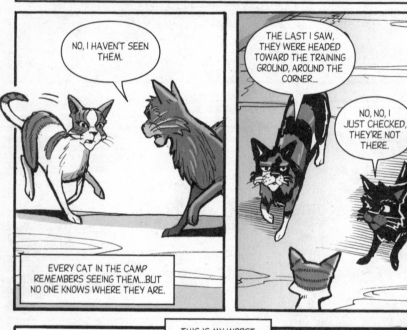

THE LAST I SAW, THEY WERE HEADED TOWARD THE TRAINING GROUND, AROUND THE CORNER...

NO, NO, I JUST CHECKED, THEY'RE NOT THERE.

THIS IS MY WORST NIGHTMARE.

I SAW THEM PLAYING WITH A STICK ON THE EDGE OF THE STREAM...

NO, THAT WAS BEFORE LEAFSTAR LEFT WITH ECHOSONG.

I TELL THE KITS I KNOW THINGS...THAT I'LL ALWAYS TAKE CARE OF THEM...

BUT THE TERRIBLE TRUTH IS...

...SOMETIMES I DON'T KNOW WHAT TO DO.

DID ANY OF YOU SEE BILLYSTORM TODAY?

NO...NOT TODAY...

NOT SINCE TWO SUNRISES AGO...

STARCLAN HELP ME.

AM I REALLY ABOUT TO ACCUSE MY MATE OF STEALING OUR KITS?

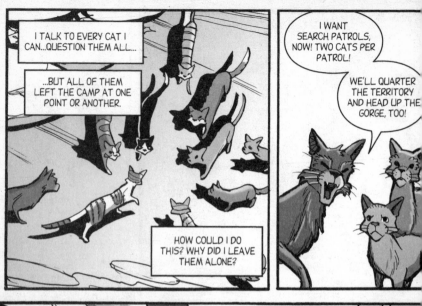

I TALK TO EVERY CAT I CAN...QUESTION THEM ALL...

...BUT ALL OF THEM LEFT THE CAMP AT ONE POINT OR ANOTHER.

HOW COULD I DO THIS? WHY DID I LEAVE THEM ALONE?

I WANT SEARCH PATROLS, NOW! TWO CATS PER PATROL!

WE'LL QUARTER THE TERRITORY AND HEAD UP THE GORGE, TOO!

STORMKIT!

HARRYKIT!

FIREKIT! CAN YOU HEAR ME?

LEAFSTAR...YOU SHOULD STAY HERE. IN CASE THE KITS COME BACK.

YOU DON'T THINK...

THEY'RE ALL RIGHT, AREN'T THEY? YOU DON'T THINK ANYTHING'S... HAPPENED...

WE'LL FIND THEM. DO YOU HEAR ME? WE WILL FIND THE KITS.

WHAT YOU ASKED US EARLIER...

DO YOU REALLY THINK BILLYSTORM HAS TAKEN THEM?

BEFORE THE FLOOD, I WOULD HAVE SAID NEVER.

BUT NOW... I DON'T KNOW.

I'LL BE RIGHT OUTSIDE.

IF YOU NEED ME.

I DON'T KNOW IF I FALL ASLEEP AS MUCH AS MY MIND JUST SHUTS DOWN...

...BUT WHEN I WAKE, NIGHT HAS FALLEN...

...AND I CAN TELL AT ONCE THAT SOMETHING ELSE HAS GONE WRONG.

EVERYONE CLEAR ON WHAT WE HAVE TO DO?

GOOD. LET'S HEAD OUT.

LEAFSTAR! SHARPCLAW'S TAKING A PATROL TO BILLYSTORM'S TWOLEG NEST!

WHAT? WHY?

WE'VE CHECKED THE WHOLE TERRITORY AND HAVEN'T FOUND THE KITS. SHARPCLAW OVERHEARD YOU ASKING ABOUT BILLYSTORM...

...AND HE THINKS BILLYSTORM'S TAKEN THEM TO TWOLEGPLACE. THEY'RE GOING THERE TO TAKE THE KITS BACK!

NO...NO, THAT'S NOT THE WAY TO DO THIS!

WELL, NO. ESPECIALLY IF THEY'RE NOT EVEN THERE.

YOU DON'T THINK BILLYSTORM TOOK THEM?

NEVER. I KNOW HOW MUCH HE LOVES YOU. HE WOULD NEVER HURT YOU LIKE THIS, NO MATTER WHAT.

WE HAVE TO STOP THAT PATROL.

WE'RE TOO LATE! WE'LL NEVER CATCH THEM!

I KNOW A SHORTCUT!

IT'LL BE FASTER IF I GO ALONE.

BUT--

NO ARGUING! STAY HERE!

STARCLAN...

...GIVE ME SPEED!

LET ME BE
IN TIME!

BILLYSTORM!

OUT FOR BLOOD, BY THE LOOKS OF IT.

SHARPCLAW!

YOU'RE WRONG! BILLYSTORM DOESN'T HAVE THE KITS!

WHAT? HOW DO YOU KNOW?

BECAUSE HE'S WITH ME.

DOESN'T HAVE THE-- *THE KITS ARE MISSING?*

SINCE THIS AFTERNOON.

THEN WHY AREN'T YOU OUT LOOKING FOR THEM? WHY WASTE TIME COMING HERE?

I WAS TRYING TO PROTECT YOU, YOU HALFWIT! SOME OF US THOUGHT YOU MIGHT'VE TAKEN THEM!

I CAN LOOK AFTER MYSELF, THANK YOU VERY MUCH!

ESPECIALLY WHEN IT COMES TO MOUSE-BRAINED PATROLS JUMPING TO DUMB CONCLUSIONS.

OH, I GUESS I SHOULD'VE JUST LET NINE WARRIORS COME AND TEAR YOU APART, THEN?

AS IF THEY COULD.

SHARPCLAW. YOU WANT TO LOOK FOR THE KITS IN MY HOUSEFOLKS' PLACE? *GO RIGHT AHEAD.*

BE MY GUEST.

58

I...DON'T SUPPOSE THAT'LL BE NECESSARY... AT THIS POINT...

LOOK, I SHOULD'VE...I MEAN, I SHOULDN'T'VE...

SAVE IT.

"RIGHT NOW THE ONLY THING I CARE ABOUT IS FINDING OUR KITS."

I JUST WANT YOU TO KNOW, LEAFSTAR, I WON'T REST UNTIL THE KITS ARE BROUGHT BACK HOME.

THEY'RE THE FUTURE OF THE CLAN. THEY'RE WARRIORS!

THANK YOU, SOL.

I APPRECIATE SOL'S WORDS, BUT THEY DON'T MAKE ME FEEL ANY BETTER.

NEITHER DOES HOW THOROUGHLY BILLYSTORM IS IGNORING ME.

DID YOU FIND THEM?

I'M GETTING MORE SEARCH PARTIES READY TO GO.

I'M SORRY, NO, I DIDN'T. BUT I'LL KEEP LOOKING.

NO...CALL THEM OFF. IF WE DON'T HUNT AND PATROL, WE'LL END UP STARVING OR ATTACKED.

YOU'RE...NOT CALLING OFF THE SEARCH, ARE YOU?

OF COURSE NOT! ECHOSONG, BILLYSTORM, AND I WILL KEEP LOOKING. I JUST--

"--I HAVE TO LOOK AFTER MY CLAN, AS WELL AS MY KITS."

FIREKIT! HARRYKIT!

STORMKIT! IT'S YOUR PAPA!

61

BILLYSTORM...I TRULY AM SORRY ABOUT THIS...

HAVE I SAID I BLAME YOU?

NO.

BUT YOU SAID THEY WOULDN'T BE SAFE IN THE GORGE, AND YOU WERE RIGHT.

LOOK, LEAFSTAR... MAYBE IT'S...

MAYBE THEY WANDERED OFF BECAUSE THEY WERE TRYING TO FIND ME.

BECAUSE I... YOU KNOW. STOPPED COMING AROUND.

THIS COULD BE ALL MY FAULT.

NO, IT'S MINE... I'M THE ONE WHO TOLD YOU TO LEAVE.

BUT I'M THEIR FATHER. I SHOULDN'T HAVE LET THAT STOP ME FROM SEEING THEM!

CAN WE SETTLE THIS LATER?

AFTER WE FIND THE KITS?

PLEASE?

ECHOSONG IS RIGHT, OF COURSE.

WE SEARCH IN SILENCE FOR A WHILE.

SILENCE FILLED WITH A MILLION THINGS I WANT TO SAY.

WHAT? WHAT IS IT?

THAT SCENT. SOL AND I SMELLED IT ON PATROL. STRANGE CATS...

AND NOW THERE'S MORE OF THEM! COME ON!

HHRRRRGGHH...

SHREWTOOTH, ARE YOU OKAY?

WERE YOU HURT LAST NIGHT?

NAH, I'M FINE.

SOL JUST KEPT ME UP, COMING AND GOING AND--

LET ME TELL YOU, I DON'T KNOW WHAT HE ROLLED IN...

...BUT I CAN STILL SMELL IT. >HAKK<

LOOK AT THIS! NO WONDER MY EYES ARE WATERING!

SOL MUST HAVE TRACKED THESE STINKY LEAVES BY MY NEST!

I'M GOING TO HAVE TO GO FOR A SWIM TO GET RID OF THIS STENCH!

HAS ANYONE SEEN SOL THIS MORNING?

I HAVEN'T.

NOPE, SORRY.

NOW, NOW, WASPWHISKER.

SOL IS VERY COMMITTED TO FINDING MY KITS.

SOL CAN STAY GONE, FAR AS I'M CONCERNED.

HRMPH. OR AN EASY SOURCE OF FOOD.

WE TAKE TURNS SENDING SEARCH PARTIES OUT OVER THE COURSE OF THE DAY.

THE ONE THING THAT GIVES ME COMFORT IS THAT I HAVEN'T SEEN ANY BUZZARDS CIRCLING OVERHEAD.

I JUST HAVE TO FIND THEM...!

SOL--HAVE YOU BEEN OUT SEARCHING AGAIN?

WELL, NO...NOT THIS TIME. I WAS TRYING TO CATCH SOME SQUIRRELS...

...BUT THEY WERE ALL TOO FAST FOR ME TODAY, I'M SORRY TO ADMIT.

MY KITS ARE ALIVE. I KNOW THEY ARE. I CAN FEEL IT.

I CAN STILL SMELL SOME OF THOSE RANK SHREWTOOTH WAS COMPLAINING ABOUT.

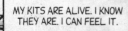

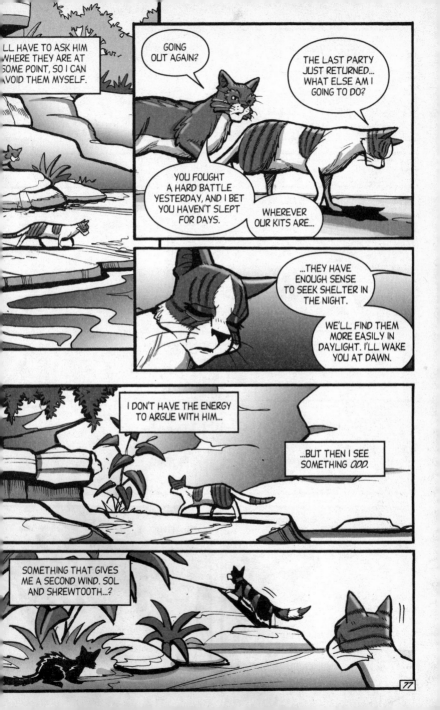

WHERE IN THE NAME OF STARCLAN COULD THEY BE GOING?

THE ABANDONED TWOLEG DEN?

WHY COME HERE?

AND WHY IN STARCLAN'S NAME IS SHREWTOOTH ACTING AS IF SOL IS PREY?

I'M BACK, LITTLE ONES.

SOL, WE'RE BORED! WHEN DO WE GET TO GO HOME?

I ALREADY TOLD YOU. LEAFSTAR DOESN'T WANT YOU BACK YET BECAUSE SHE'S STILL REBUILDING YOUR DEN.

AWWWW...

NOW, CAN SOMEONE TELL ME WHY YOU HAVEN'T EATEN THE MOUSE I BROUGHT YOU?

WE DON'T LIKE IT. THE ONES MAMA CATCHES TASTE BETTER.

I BANISH YOU FROM SKYCLAN.

YOU'VE BETRAYED MY TRUST, BETRAYED THE WARRIOR CODE...

...BETRAYED EVERYTHING I THOUGHT YOU BELIEVED IN.

OH, JUST BECAUSE YOU SAY IT, THAT MAKES IT SO, DOES IT?

WELL LET ME TELL YOU A FEW THINGS, LEAFSTAR. I--

GO AHEAD, SOL.

TELL US HOW THINGS ARE GOING TO BE.

I...I...

I'LL TELL YOU. YOU'RE LEAVING, SOL. YOU'RE GOING FAR AWAY.

AND YOU'RE NOT EVER COMING BACK.

YOU. YOU HAVE NO RIGHT TO SPEAK HERE.

YOU MAKE ME SICK.

PATHETIC "DAYLIGHT WARRIOR," ALWAYS TROTTING BACK TO YOUR TWOLEGS WHEN IT GETS DARK AND COLD.

NOT ANYMORE.

MY PLACE IS IN THE GORGE FROM NOW ON. MY FAMILY NEEDS ME, AND THIS IS WHERE I BELONG.

THE CLAN UNITED AGAINST THOSE ROGUES.

WE PROVED THAT NO CAT IS GOING TO LEAVE THE GORGE, NOT UNTIL STARCLAN CALLS THEM.

IF THE FUTURE OF SKYCLAN IS HERE, THEN SO IS MINE.

BILLYSTORM... ARE YOU SURE?

NEVER MORE SO.

ERIN HUNTER

is inspired by a love of cats and a fascination with the ferocity of the natural world. As well as having great respect for nature in all its forms, Erin enjoys creating rich, mythical explanations for animal behavior. She is also the author of the bestselling Seekers series.

Download the free Warriors app and chat on Warriors message boards at www.warriorcats.com.

For exclusive information on your favorite authors and artists, visit www.authortracker.com.

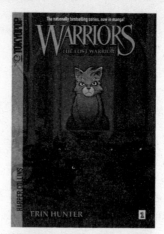

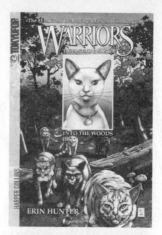

Sasha has everything she wants: kind housefolk who take care of her during the day, and the freedom to explore the woods beyond Twolegplace at night. But when Sasha is forced to leave her home, she must forge a solitary new life in the forest. When Sasha meets Tigerstar, leader of ShadowClan, she begins to think that she may be better off joining the ranks of his forest Clan. But Tigerstar has many secrets, and Sasha must decide whether she can trust him.

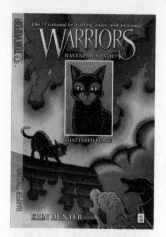

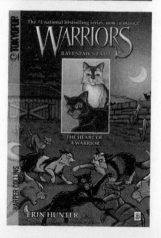

RAVENPAW FIGHTS
TO DEFEND HIS HOME IN

WARRIORS

RAVENPAW'S
PATH

#1: SHATTERED PEACE

#2: A CLAN IN NEED

#3: THE HEART OF A WARRIOR

Ravenpaw has settled into life on the farm, away from the forest and Tigerstar's evil eye. He knows that leaving the warrior Clans was the right choice, and he appreciates his quiet days and peaceful nights with his best friend, Barley. But when five rogue cats from Twolegplace come to the barn seeking shelter, Ravenpaw and Barley are forced to flee their new home. With the help of ThunderClan, Ravenpaw and Barley must try to find a way to overpower the rogues—before they lose their home for good.

TOKYOPOP®

WARRIORS

THE RISE OF SCOURGE

HARPER COLLINS

ERIN HUNTER

WARRIORS

THE RISE OF SCOURGE

Black-and-white Tiny may be the runt of the litter, but he's also the most curious about what lies beyond the backyard fence. When he crosses paths with some wild cats defending their territory, Tiny is left with scars—and a bitter, deep-seated grudge—that he carries with him back to Twolegplace. As his reputation grows among the strays and loners that live in the dirty brick alleyways, Tiny leaves behind his name, his kittypet past, and everything that was once important to him—except his deadly desire for revenge.

THE #1 NATIONAL BESTSELLING SERIES

OMEN OF THE STARS

WARRIORS

THE LAST HOPE

ADVENTURE
GAME
INSIDE!

ERIN HUNTER

TURN THE PAGE FOR A PEEK
AT THE NEXT WARRIORS NOVEL,

WARRIORS

OMEN OF
THE STARS #6

THE LAST HOPE

The battle between the Dark Forest and the warrior Clans has come. As the cats seek out their allies and enemies, Jayfeather, Lionblaze, and Dovewing wait desperately for the fourth cat who is prophesied to help them lead the Clans to victory—and who may be their only hope for survival.

CHAPTER 1

❧

Someone's bleeding!

Ivypool stiffened as the memory of Antpelt's death flooded her mind, just as it always did when the scent of blood hit her. She could still feel his flesh tearing beneath her claws, still see his final agonized spasm before he stopped moving forever. She'd been forced to kill the WindClan warrior to convince Tigerstar of her loyalty. It had earned her the grim honor of training Dark Forest warriors, but she knew she would never wash the scent of his blood from her paws.

"Stop!" she yowled.

Birchfall froze mid-lunge and stared at her. "What's wrong?"

"I smell blood," she snapped. "We're only training. I don't want any injuries."

Birchfall blinked at her, puzzled.

Redwillow scrambled up from underneath Birchfall's paws. "It's just a nick," the ShadowClan warrior meowed. He showed Ivypool his ear. Blood welled from a thin scratch at the tip.

"Just be careful," Ivypool cautioned.

"*Be careful?*" Hawkfrost's snarl made her spin around. "There's a war coming and it won't be won with sheathed claws." The Dark Forest warrior was circling the dingy clearing. Shadowy trunks, slick with moss, loomed around him. Hawkfrost curled his lip and stared at Ivypool. "I thought you were helping to train our recruits to fight like real warriors, not soft Clan cats."

Birchfall bristled. "Clan cats aren't soft!"

"Then why do you come here?" Hawkfrost challenged.

Redwillow whisked his tail. "Our Clans need us to be the best warriors we can be. You told us that, remember?"

Hawkfrost nodded slowly. "And you can only learn the skills you need *here*." He flicked his nose toward Birchfall. "Attack Redwillow again," he ordered. "This time don't stop at the first scent of blood." He narrowed his eyes at Ivypool.

Ivypool swallowed, terrified she'd given herself away. No Dark Forest cat could ever know that she came here to spy for Dovewing, Jayfeather, and Lionblaze. Growling, she lifted her chin and barged past Birchfall. "Do it like this," she told him. With a hiss she hurled herself at Redwillow, ducking away from his claws, and grasped his forepaw between her jaws. Using his weight to unbalance him, she snapped her head around and twisted him deftly onto his back. He landed with a thump, which she knew sounded more painful than it felt. She'd hardly pierced his fur with her teeth and her jerk was so well-timed it had knocked him off his feet without wrenching his leg.

She glanced back at Hawkfrost, relieved to see approval glinting in his eyes. He'd only seen the flash of fur and claw and heard the smack of muscle against the slippery earth.

Redwillow jumped to his paws. "Can I try that on Birchfall?"

Ivypool sniffed. "Of course." She padded to join Hawkfrost and watched Redwillow fly at Birchfall.

"Nice move." Hawkfrost growled in her ear as Redwillow tore a lump of fur from Birchfall's shoulder. Birchfall yowled and spun on his haunches. He stretched up his head, ready to lunge.

"He's left his throat vulnerable." Hawkfrost leaned forward, ears pricking. He sounded eager, hungry for a fatal blow.

No! Ivypool dug her claws into the ground to stop herself from leaping between the warriors as Redwillow sprang forward, his teeth snapping toward Birchfall's neck. Birchfall reared up just in time and snagged Redwillow's muzzle with hooked claws.

"Hawkfrost!"

Birchfall and Redwillow stumbled to a halt as

Applefur appeared from the mist. The ShadowClan she-cat's eyes were bright, her mottled brown pelt pulsing with heat from training. "Blossomfall and Hollowflight want to fight *Dark Forest* warriors."

Applefur's apprentices padded out of the shadows. "We can fight Clan cats anytime," Blossomfall complained.

Hollowflight nodded. "We come here to learn skills we can't learn anywhere else." The RiverClan tom's pelt was matted with blood. Clumps of fur stuck out along his spine.

Haven't you had enough? Ivypool glanced at Hawkfrost. "Are there any Dark Forest warriors close by?" she ventured, praying there weren't.

"Of course." Hawkfrost tasted the air.

The screech of fighting cats echoed through the mist. It had become like birdsong to Ivypool—filling the forest, so familiar that she only heard it when she listened for it. "Why aren't we training with them tonight?" she asked. Most nights, the Dark Forest warriors couldn't wait to share their cruel skills with the Clan cats.

Hawkfrost wove between Blossomfall and Applefur. "I want you to learn how other Clans fight."

Ivypool shivered.

"You may be fighting side by side one day," Hawkfrost went on.

Liar!

"You need to know your allies' moves so you can match them, claw for claw."

No, you're training them to destroy one another in the final battle.

A husky growl echoed from the trees. "Four Clans will unite as one when it matters most." Tigerstar padded from the shadows, his wide tabby head held high. "This is the law of the Dark Forest. Remember it."

Birchfall nodded solemnly. "Four Clans will unite as one when it matters most," he echoed.

"When will that be?" Blossomfall's eyes were round.

"You'll know when the time comes." Mapleshade slunk from the trees. Her tortoiseshell pelt was so transparent now that the white patches showed the forest behind. Ivypool flinched at the reminder that she too would fade from every memory one day.

"Tigerstar?" Blossomfall was staring at the dark warrior. "Are we training for something special?"

Ivypool flinched. "Not yet," she meowed quickly, one eye on Tigerstar. He nodded and she went on. "But you never know." She remembered the vicious battle with WindClan in the tunnels only a quarter moon earlier. "There may be more cats like Sol ready to lead one Clan against another."

Applefur stepped forward. "Next time a rogue tries to drive us apart, I'll stand beside ThunderClan, not against them!"

Ivypool shifted her paws. *These cats believe their loyalty to the Clans is being strengthened.* She glanced at Birchfall. *But who will they be loyal to when the final battle comes? Their Clanmates or the Dark Forest warriors?*

ENTER THE WORLD OF
WARRIORS

Warriors

Sinister perils threaten the four warrior Clans. Into the midst of this turmoil comes Rusty, an ordinary housecat, who may just be the bravest of them all.

Download the new free Warriors app at www.warriorcats.com

Warriors: The New Prophecy

Follow the next generation of heroic cats as they set off on a quest to save the Clans from destruction.

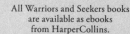

All Warriors and Seekers books are available as ebooks from HarperCollins.

 Also available unabridged from HarperChildren's *Audio*

HARPER
An Imprint of HarperCollins Publishers

Visit www.warriorcats.com for the free Warriors app, games, Clan lore, and much more!

Warriors: Power of Three

Firestar's grandchildren begin their training as warrior cats.
Prophecy foretells that they will hold more power than any cats before them.

Warriors: Omen of the Stars

Which ThunderClan apprentice will complete the prophecy that
foretells that three Clanmates hold the future of the Clans in their paws?

HARPER
An Imprint of HarperCollinsPublishers

Also available unabridged from HarperChildren's*Audio*

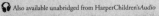

Visit www.warriorcats.com for the free Warriors app, games, Clan lore, and much more!

Delve Deeper into the Clans

Warrior Cats Come to Life in Manga!

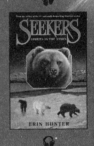